Pirate Stories for Little Children

Pirate Stories for Little Children

Russell Punter

Illustrated by Benji Davies,
Christyan Fox, Desideria Guicciardini
and Kate Sheppard

Contents

4

Pirates Ahoy!

"Wait for me!" yelled Ben Buckle. He was a cabin boy aboard *The Jolly Rascal*.

His ship was about
to set sail on a hunt
for treasure.

As the ship left port, Ben took
Captain Cutlass his sea charts.

Thank'ee, boy!

The ship sailed
all day and into
the starry night.

Ben felt the sea getting rougher and rougher.

Suddenly, they were
in the middle of a
massive storm.

The ship lurched
from side to side.

Huge waves crashed
onto the deck.

Ben clung to the mast in
panic. "I hope we don't
capsize!" he thought.

At last, the storm blew itself out, and the pirates started patching up the sails.

This will take some mending!

Meanwhile, Ben was at his look-out post when he spotted something...

Ship ahoy!

Prepare to attack, lads!

The crew loaded the cannons
and took aim.

BOOM! roared one.

BA-BOOM!
blasted another.

Ha har!

Ow, my
ears!

Ben watched as Captain Cutlass and the crew leaped aboard the other ship.

Swords clanged.

Sailors yelped.

Pirates yelled.

Take 'em alive, lads!

Yikes!

Help!

"We've won!" called Captain Cutlass.
Ben helped the pirates haul
the treasure chests on deck.

Fancy!

Sparkly!

Here's another one!

Caw! Pieces of eight!

Ben had never seen so many glittering gold doubloons.

Wow!

The ship's crew was
put into a boat…

and brought aboard
The Jolly Rascal.

"Don't worry," said Captain Cutlass.
"We'll put you ashore at the next island."

Caw!
Welcome aboard!

After dropping off the sailors, the pirates had a party.
The ship shook with sea shanties and jolly jigs, until...

Ben and the others
scrambled on deck.

Soon *The Jolly Rascal*
was racing through
the water.

Full speed
ahead, lads!

They hid in a sheltered cove as the pirate hunters sailed past.

"We escaped!" gasped Ben in relief.

"On to our next adventure!" cried Captain Cutlass.

The Pesky Parrot

Charlie Crossbones had just left Pirate School.

He knew how to read a map...

unlock a treasure chest...

raise **The Jolly Roger**...

and do a proper pirate's laugh.

Ha..har..har!

He had all he needed to
be a pirate.

Except for one thing...

And then, down by the docks, Charlie found parrots galore.

USED PARROT SALE

Get the bird here!

Parrots going cheap!

To his dismay, the parrots were all
far too expensive.

Then the parrot seller took pity on him.

"There is one bird you could have," he said.

You've got a very special bird there.

Charlie had never seen such a pretty parrot – and it only cost a penny.

going cheap

Now Charlie and his parrot could sail the Seven Seas in search of treasure.

Out at sea, Charlie soon spotted a ship he recognized –
The Fat Flounder, belonging to Captain Silverside.

Charlie slipped into his rowing boat. Quickly and quietly, he rowed over to the ship.

Then he sneaked in through an open window.

He was in luck. He'd found the captain's treasure cabin.

But, as he stuffed his pockets with jewels,
disaster struck!

Stop thief!

"Sssh!" Charlie hissed at his parrot.
It was too late.

Captain Silverside and his crew chased Charlie around the deck six times.

Come back, you sneaky thief!

Puffing and panting, Charlie only just escaped to his boat.

Charlie turned to his parrot with a
face like thunder.

Don't ever do
that again, you
pesky parrot!

But every time they went to sea, the
parrot caused trouble.

Just as Charlie was about to steal
someone's treasure...

...the parrot let out a warning screech.

Charlie had had enough.

He tried to get rid of
the parrot...

...but it always flew back
to his shoulder.

So Charlie went to the local inn for
dinner, to cheer himself up.

The Laughing Lobster Inn
Super Deluxe Menu
Scrummy Scampi 7 pennies
Mouthwatering Mussels 6 pennies
Deluxe Menu
Crispy Cod 5 pennies
Fancy Fishcakes 4 pennies
Cheap Menu
Shrimp on toast 3 pennies
Very Cheap Menu
Bread and cheese 1 penny
(free jug of water with all orders)

Thanks to that pesky parrot, he only had
enough money for bread and cheese.

While Charlie was talking to
Mr. Grog, the innkeeper...

...a thief was creeping up
to Mr. Grog's cash box.

The crook was about to strike, when Charlie's parrot squawked into action.

Stop thief!

"What a wonderful bird!" said Mr. Grog.

"That thief nearly got away with my cash."

This gave Charlie an idea.
He sold his parrot to the innkeeper.

Mr. Grog was delighted with his new burglar alarm...

Stop thief!

the parrot enjoyed its new job...

...and Charlie bought another bird – a quiet one this time!

Captain Spike

Macintosh Mullet was a poor, poor fisherman.

He lived on tiny Mullet Island with his only daughter, Molly.

One morning, Macintosh gave a sad sigh.

He hadn't caught any fish for a month.

Molly packed their valuables into
a chest and left for the mainland.

Less than ten minutes later, Molly was grabbed by Captain Spike and his band of pirates.

Spike tried everything to find out where Molly had hidden the key to the chest.

He tickled her.

Yuck!

He fed her stale ship's biscuits.

SHIP'S BISCUITS

Molly refused to talk.

Spike was losing patience, when a thick fog swirled around the ship.

"Help! Where are we? We can't see," wailed the pirates.

"I know these waters," said Molly. "I'll guide you home... if you let me go afterwards."

Done! Shark Island, and step on it!

After an hour, the fog began to clear.

"I'll take over from here," boomed Spike.
"YOU can walk the plank!"

Spike made Molly walk off a plank...

into the shark-filled sea.

But, instead of a **splash**, all the pirates heard
was a thud!

At that moment, the last of the fog lifted.

"This isn't Shark Island!" growled Spike.

"We've been tricked!"

Molly had steered them into port.

The port police carried off the pirates to jail.

And clever Molly carried off a **big** reward.

Percy and the Pirates

Percy Pike lived with his family by the sea.

Most of the time he was happy.

But not at meal times.

There was never enough to eat.

Percy's tummy often rumbled all day long.

So Percy made a plan.

He borrowed his dad's boat and rowed out to sea.

Dangling his fishing rod over the side,
he waited for the fish to bite.

But all he got was a leak...

in the bottom of his boat.

Luckily, he was rescued by a passing ship.

Unluckily, it was a passing pirate ship.

"I'm Captain Crook and this is my crew!"
bellowed a red-faced man.

My name's
Percy Pike.

"Tell Percy what we do on this ship, lads,"
Captain Crook barked.

The three crew members burst into song...

We steal for Crook, 'cos he's the best,

Then put the treasure in his chest.

"Or else you'll walk the plank," said Crook.

Percy didn't want to
be a pirate...

but he didn't want to be
shark food either.

"Ship ahoy!" shouted a pirate.

"Board her, boys!" ordered Captain Crook.

The three pirates swung
across to the other ship...

chased her crew
around the deck...

and came back with bags
bursting with gold, silver
and diamonds.

The pirates poured the treasure into
Captain Crook's chest.

Well, almost all the treasure...

That night, Crook found gold
in Sam Scurvy's locker...

diamonds under Willy
Weevil's bunk...

...and silver in Ronnie
Rum's spare sea boots.

"No one steals from me!" growled Captain Crook.

The double-crossing pirates were forced to walk the plank.

Percy was the only one left.

"We're going on a night raid," said Crook.

"And no tricks when we get on
that ship," he warned.

While the crew of the ship snored in their bunks,
Percy searched the cabins.

Instead of treasure, he only found maps –
but they gave him a brilliant idea.

He grabbed a quill, and
picked out a map of a
nearby island.

First, he drew a wiggly
arrow across the island.

Then he added an 'X' at the
end of the arrow.

Last of all, he wrote
'treasure' underneath
the 'X'.

Percy crept out to Captain Crook with the map.
"I found a treasure map," he whispered.

"Ha!" said Crook, snatching it.

"Soon I'll be rich!" he crowed,
as they rowed back to his ship.

At dawn, they reached the island on the map.

They followed
Percy's arrow, past
palm trees...

between
spiky rocks...

around a
lake...

and over a
rushing river...

X

until they
reached the
'X'.

"Give me that shovel, boy!" yelled the captain.

Crook began digging furiously.

Soon he was
deep, deep down
underground.

"Just you wait until I get out of here!"
Captain Crook screamed at Percy.

But however hard he tried...

he couldn't
climb out.

Percy took his chance.

"Cheerio, Captain!" he shouted, and
he ran back to the pirate ship.

Percy lowered the Jolly Roger and set sail.
In no time he was cruising into his home port.

Percy returned Crook's booty to its owners.

They were so grateful, they gave him his very own bulging treasure chest as a reward.

Percy arrived home a hero.

And the Pike family never went hungry again.

The Cabin Boy's Secret

Harriet Hill and her parents owned a sheep farm by the sea.

They were poor, but they had a happy life, until one day...

...Sir Rollo Pinchly, the sea trader
burst into the farmhouse.

He flung a tiny bag of coins at Harriet's dad.

"I want to buy this place," bellowed Pinchly.

"We'd never sell our farm," replied Mr. Hill.

"I need your land for a new dockyard,"
roared Pinchly, storming off.

"...I'll get it, somehow!"

The next day, disaster struck.

"Our sheep have vanished,"
cried Mr. Hill.

"We're ruined," sobbed his wife.
"Now we'll have to sell the farm."

"Don't worry," said Harriet. "I'll find a job and earn enough money to buy more sheep."

So she packed some clothes and headed into town.

But when she arrived, there were no jobs anywhere.

Then she spotted a sign by an old, creaky galleon at the dockside...

Cabin boy
wanted – apply at
The Salty Seadog

The Salty Seadog

"I need that job," thought Harriet.

She hid behind some barrels and untied her bundle of clothes.

"One cabin boy coming up," she thought.

She slipped on a pair of baggy shorts...

...hid her long curly hair under a spotted headscarf...

...and tugged on a big striped shirt.

Minutes later, she was in the captain's cabin.

"I'm Harry, and I want to be a cabin boy," she said gruffly.

"Hmmm..." said Captain Scuttle, thoughtfully.

"You're a little skinny, but you'll do. Welcome aboard, lad!"

The ship set sail and Harriet began her training.

Clash!

Clang!

There were sword fighting classes...

...and lessons on blasting locks off treasure chests.

BANG!

There were even lessons on walking the plank.

Harriet soon realized that the crew of *The Salty Seadog* were no ordinary sailors - they were pirates!

But it was too late to jump ship now.

Harriet would just have to try
and steer clear of trouble.

One morning, a
cry went out from
Hawkeye Henry,
high up in the
crow's nest...

SHIP AHOY, ME HEARTIES!

Captain Scuttle grabbed his telescope.

"That ship's deck is packed with goodies," he shouted excitedly.

"Let's board her and grab 'em lads!

You stay and steer our ship, Harry."

Harriet watched the pirates
swing across to the ship...

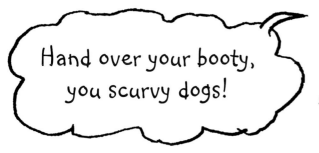

Hand over your booty,
you scurvy dogs!

...and chase the crew
around the deck.

In no time, the crew were rounded up and tied together.

"Well done lads!" chuckled Captain Scuttle.

"Now let's help ourselves to the booty."

But the pirates' luck was about to run out.

Whooosh! A heavy sail fell from above, swamping the captain and his men.

Harriet gasped when she saw who had dropped the sail...

"Sir Rollo Pinchly!"

Pinchly locked up the pirates. Then he marched his crew below decks for a talking to.

"Now's my chance," thought Harriet. She swung across to the other ship...

tip-toed across the deck...

slid back the bolt on the cabin door...

and freed her friends.

Thank'ee, lad!

"Back to the *Seadog*, boys!" whispered Scuttle.

Just then, Harriet heard a familiar sound…

"I recognize those curly coats!" thought Harriet.

The noise brought Pinchly and his men racing on deck.

"Hands off my cargo!" yelled Pinchly.

"They're my sheep, not yours!" cried Harriet.

When Harriet told her tale, Captain Scuttle was furious.

"Not even pirates steal from poor folk!" he barked.

"Seize this ruffian, men!"
ordered Pinchly.

But Pinchly's crew were as shocked as Scuttle.

"We never knew the sheep were stolen."

They wound a clanking chain around Pinchly.

"You'll be flung in jail when we reach port," said a sailor.

Harriet persuaded Pinchly's men
to let the pirates go free.

"After all, they did find my sheep," she said.

"Three cheers for Harry, er, Harriet, me hearties!" yelled Scuttle, as they sailed to Curly Fleece Farm.

Harriet was looking forward to being back on dry land.

But she'd never forget her exciting time as a swashbuckling pirate.

Pirate of the Year

T
oday was the final of the
Pirate of the Year contest.

There were only two contestants left – Captain
Blackheart and Billy Booty.

The lucky winner would receive a chest full of treasure.

Ye scoreboard

Blackheart   Billy

Rules

1. Cheating is expected. (Just don't get caught.)

2. Pirates **must** protect each other against danger.

Task one was a flat-out galleon race to Skull Island and back.

Ear-splitting cannon fire started them off.

Billy quickly took the lead.

But as soon as the ships were out of sight of the judges, Blackheart got to work.

Flaps opened in his ship's hull,
and ten oars shot out.

"All right, lads," he cried to his crew.
"Start rowing!"

"Cheat!" yelled Billy, as Blackheart raced by.

"Remember rule one!" laughed Blackheart.

When the judges came in sight,
Blackheart's crew whipped in their oars.

"I win!" cried Blackheart, crossing the finish line with a whoop.

Blackheart | Billy
1 | 0

Next, they had to dive for a silver chest.

Blackheart gave Billy a big hug. "Good luck, matey!" he boomed.

The pirates plunged into the water and

dived down, down, down...

to the seabed.

Billy grabbed the chest and was heading back when...

...three sharks appeared from nowhere and surrounded him, grinning fiercely.

Billy dropped the chest and swam for his life.

Seconds later, Blackheart surfaced triumphantly, clutching the chest himself.

Blackheart	Billy
2	0

Billy felt something slimy in his swimsuit pocket.
"So that's why Blackheart hugged me," he thought.

He knew the sharks would come after this.

Parrot training was next. The pirate with the chattiest bird would triumph.

Billy's parrot, Mimi, went first.

Pieces of eight!

Ship ahoy!

Pretty boy!

"Beat that, Blackheart!" said Billy, with a smile.

"Ha!" scoffed his opponent. "Wait until you hear my bird, Hook Beak."

"Hook Beak's the winner!" declared a judge.

Only Blackheart knew that it was one of his crew who'd really done the talking.

Blackheart 3   Billy 0

With Blackheart in the lead, it was time for the final task.

On the shore of Skull Island,
each pirate was given a map.

The first one to find their buried
treasure chest would win.

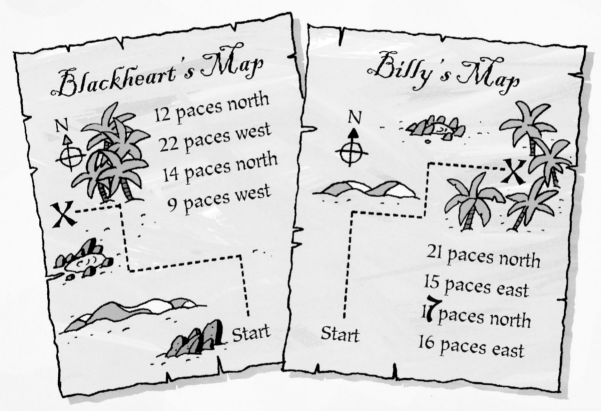

Blackheart's Map

N

12 paces north
22 paces west
14 paces north
9 paces west

X

Start

Billy's Map

N

X

21 paces north
15 paces east
17 paces north
16 paces east

Start

There was something odd about Billy's map
– but he had no time to hesitate.

The pirates paced out their routes.

But Billy forgot to look where he was going.

...15, 16...

He walked straight into a rock pool full of angry crabs.

17... ouch!

"Blackheart added six extra paces to my map," thought Billy, as crazy crabs pinched him all over.

Meanwhile, Blackheart had found his chest and bounded across the beach to show the judges.

"I win... aaagh!" he yelped. "Help me! Quick! I'm sinking in quicksand."

Billy snapped a branch from a palm tree. "Grab this!" he called.

Hauling and heaving, he dragged his rival to safety.

"Well done, Billy!" cheered the crowd.

"I still won the task," sniffed the ungrateful Blackheart.

"One point for Blackheart," agreed the judges.
"But five bonus points to Billy for saving his life."

"Pirate of the Year!" squawked
Mimi proudly, as Billy was
given the prize.

Blackheart	Billy
4	5

The Ghostly Galleon

Harmony the mermaid lived at the bottom of the ocean.

She spent every morning collecting shells and starfish.

Then she took them back to her
mother to make their tiny, dark cave
more cheerful.

This will brighten up
the place.

They were too poor to afford a better home.

Harmony tried to keep their spirits up by singing beautiful songs.

Her voice was so lovely, passing fish would stop and listen.

One day, Harmony's mother came
out in splotchy blue spots.

Will she be
all right?

Say 'ahh!'

Dr. Finley examined her from top to tail.

"Your mother is very sick," he said.

"The only cure is polkadot seaweed,
taken twice a day for one week."

"I'll swim off right now to find some," said Harmony.

Dr. Finley sighed. "It only grows in the Pirates' Graveyard."

"Not the spooky place full of sunken pirate ships?" gasped Harmony.

"Yes. And it's haunted by the ghost of Gingerbeard – the fiercest pirate who ever lived."

Harmony was terrified. But she had to find that seaweed.

She swam for hours until she reached the
creepy Pirates' Graveyard.

After a long search among the sinister wrecks,
something spotted caught her eye.

Polkadot seaweed!
At last!

"Stop right there!" boomed a spine-chilling voice.

Come to steal my gold, have ye?

Gi- Gi- Gingerbeard's ghost!

"I just need polkadot seaweed for my mother," explained Harmony, "not your treasure."

A likely tale! There's something fishy about you.

Ow!

The ghostly pirate locked Harmony in a gloomy cabin on his ship.

"Who will help my mother now?"
sighed Harmony sadly.

She tried to cheer herself up by singing.

But she was so miserable, all her
songs came out sounding sad.

The tragic tunes drifted up on
deck, where Gingerbeard was
on patrol.

However hard he tried, the pirate couldn't help listening to the sad songs.

On Monday, they made him feel glum.

When he took Harmony some food on Tuesday, he was even more down-hearted.

By Wednesday lunchtime, even his beard
was starting to droop with despair.

Come Thursday, the songs had made him so
sorry he could hardly speak.

By Friday, Gingerbeard couldn't take any more.

"Take this chest and go!" he wailed.

Harmony swam home at full speed with the polkadot seaweed.

But seaweed wasn't the only thing in the chest. It was full of gold coins too.

So Harmony's mother was cured...

...and the happy mermaids moved into a bright, roomy new cave.

The Masked Pirate

WANTED

The Masked Pirate
BIG REWARD!

S am Sardine dreamed of
becoming a sailor.

He wanted to explore the Seven Seas, and do
battle with bloodthirsty pirates.

So he joined Captain Winkle's crew.

But life on board ship wasn't as thrilling
as Sam had hoped.

He spent all day
mopping the decks...

peeling potatoes...

and washing the sailors'
smelly socks.

After a month, Sam asked the captain
for a more exciting job.

"All right then," said Captain Winkle.
"Let's see you sail the ship into port."

Sam's chest swelled with pride as he took the wheel.

But steering a ship wasn't as easy as it looked...

"Um, maybe I should start with something simpler," said Sam.

Captain Winkle agreed.

He told Sam to guard the ship's treasure while the crew slept.

But Sam was so tired after sailing the ship, that he drifted...

Zzzzz!

off...

to...

sleep.

The next morning, Sam was woken by a wicked laugh.

The dreaded Masked Pirate had sneaked in and stolen the captain's treasure!

When the captain heard, he was not too happy.

After he'd calmed down, he offered a reward to whoever found the thief or his treasure.

But no one knew what the Masked Pirate looked like without his disguise.

Then Sam smiled. He'd had an idea.

He left at once to spend the night at The Spyglass Inn, which was always full of pirates.

The next morning over breakfast,
Sam announced,

"I heard the Masked Pirate talking
in his sleep last night."

One particular pirate frowned at Sam.

Sam's plan was working.

"Now I know where the treasure is, I'll get it for myself," said Sam.

The worried looking pirate shot out of the inn like lightning.

Sam followed close behind.

The pirate jumped into a boat and rowed as fast as he could to a nearby island.

Sam raced to Captain Winkle.

"Follow that pirate!" he cried.

On the island, the pirate
was heaving a treasure
chest out of the sand.

Captain Winkle recognized it at once. It was his chest!

"Take my ship and get help," he shouted.

The reward money is yours Sam!

"You trust me to sail?" said Sam, with a sharp salute. That was the best reward of all.

The Return of Captain Spike

O n the shore of Rotter's Isle stood
a gloomy old castle.

But this was no ordinary castle. It
was a prison – for pirates!

Once a month, a ship
full of prisoners arrived.

HMS Con Carrier

The pirates were marched ashore and thrown into the dark, dank dungeons.

No one had ever escaped from Rotter's Isle.

The newest prisoner was selfish
Captain Spike.

He was so mean, even other pirates hated him.

From the day Spike arrived, things went missing.

Cut-throat Craig's pocket watch disappeared.

Roger Redbeard's silver earring vanished in the night.

And Sidney Skull lost his gold locket.

No one knew who the thief was.

But Bobby Bones noticed Spike's booty bag getting fuller and fuller...

When Spike wasn't sneaking around, he was busy showing off.

"No jail can hold me!" he bragged. "I'm going to escape."

"Ha!" laughed Bobby Bones.
"I bet you'll be back in twenty-four hours."

"What do you bet?" asked Spike.

"My treasure map," replied Bobby.
"Stay out for more than a day, and I'll
send it to you."

"You're on!" agreed Spike.

"Address it to The Spyglass Inn," said Spike confidently. "It'll reach me there."

"But if you fail," said Bobby,
"I get everything in your booty bag."

Spike couldn't wait to get his hands on the map.

That night, he took it from under Bobby's pillow.

He unlocked the cell door with a stolen key.

Then he crept past the guards and down to the dock.

Stealing a small boat, he set sail.

Using the stars to guide him, Spike followed the directions on Bobby's treasure map.

As it got light, Spike saw land.

"That must be the island on the map," he thought.

Once ashore, he followed the directions to the treasure...

"Yippee! I'll soon be rich!" he yelled.

Spike took a shovel from his bag
and began digging.

"Bobby Bones was a fool to tell me about his map!" laughed
the treacherous pirate.

Spike dug **deeper**...

and **deeper**...

and **deeper**.

He shook with excitement as the ground moved beneath him. "This is it!" he cried.

The next moment, Spike tumbled downward
and landed bump! on a cold, stone floor.

"Welcome back!" shouted Bobby Bones.

Silly Spike had fallen for Bobby's trick.

He had sailed right around Rotter's Isle and was back where he started.

With thanks to Sarah Courtauld

Edited by Jenny Tyler and Lesley Sims

First published in 2014 by Usborne Publishing Ltd., Usborne House, 83-85 Saffron Hill, London EC1N 8RT, England. www.usborne.com
Copyright © 2014 Usborne Publishing Ltd.